THE LAUGHING DRAGON

KENNETH MAHOOD

CHARLES SCRIBNER'S SONS

NEW YORK

On a cold autumn morning a long time ago the Emperor of Japan was about to eat his morning egg when suddenly . . .

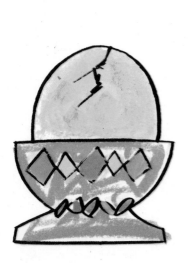

SNAP! . . .   CRACKLE! . . .   POP!

. . . out jumped a little smiling dragon.

He seemed very friendly, so the Emperor decided to call him Hojo and keep him as the Imperial Pet. Hojo soon became a great favorite with everyone by making himself useful around the palace. He made delicious soups, had a very light hand with pastry, and the Emperor loved his pancakes. In addition he was always gay and cheerful, could sing, play chess, enjoy a joke, and his hot breath kept the palace warm, which was a great comfort to the Emperor who suffered from cold feet.

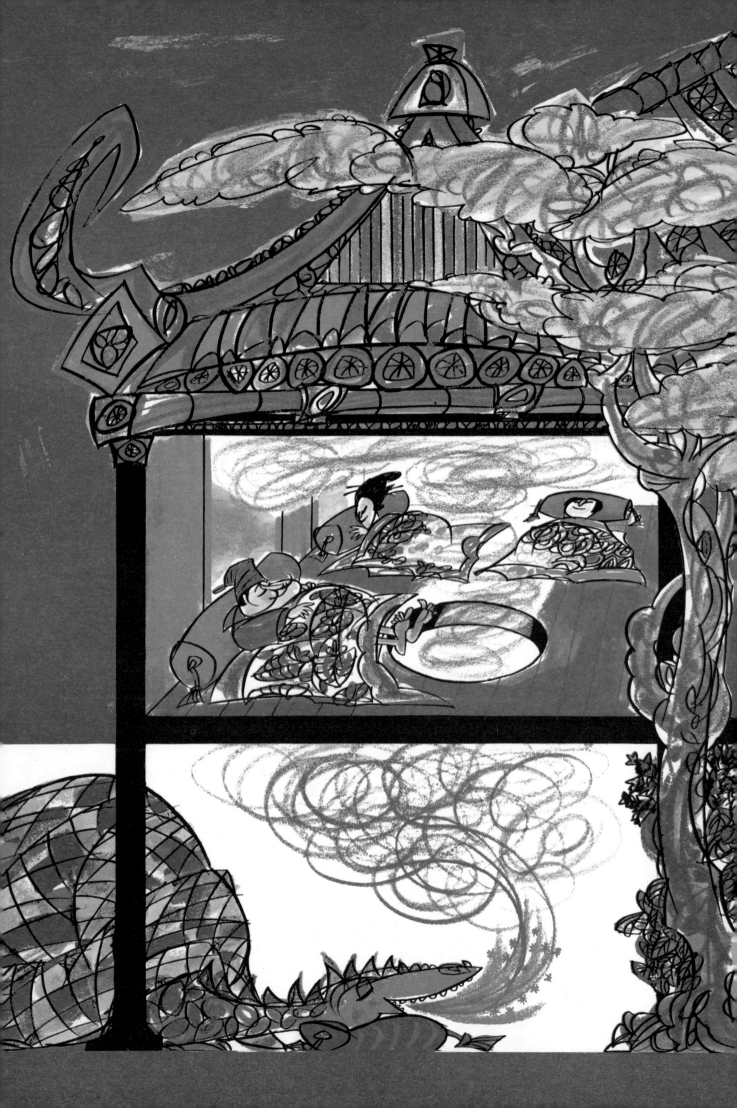

Hojo's hot breath was a mixed blessing, however, for every time he laughed, flames shot in all directions. When anyone complained, the Emperor always replied, "It's nothing, his breath is worse than his bite."

As Hojo grew bigger and bigger his breath became hotter and hotter, and more and more people got burnt. At last a group of courtiers, still smouldering, appealed to the Emperor for help. "He must be cured before we are all burnt to a cinder," they cried. So the Emperor sent for the Imperial Physician.

The Imperial Physician fitted Hojo with a muzzle but that didn't work. He tried to put the flames out with buckets and buckets of medicine but it all turned to steam. Finally, he gave

him hundreds of anti-laughing pills but they only turned red hot in his stomach. He coughed them out and laughed more than ever.

Although the Emperor had cold feet he had a warm heart and wanted to keep Hojo despite his flame-throwing habit; but when the Palace caught fire, he had to give the order for Hojo to be sent to some place where he could do no harm. "I hate to do this," he called, "but your trouble is that you can only see the funny side of life."

Hojo was left
on a bleak fireproof island
far away from Japan, the Emperor,
and all his friends. It wasn't true,
he thought, that if you laughed
the whole world laughed
with you.

BEWARE
LAUGHING
DRAGON

Hojo was feeling very doleful when he met a turtle called George: "Who's the laughing dragon?" he asked. "I am," replied Hojo. "You mean you were," said George. "I have never seen anyone so gloomy." "You would be sad if you were sent to an island just because of laughing too much," said Hojo, and told George the whole story. "You should always look before you laugh," murmured George, and ducked into his shell as Hojo started to chuckle.

BEWARE
LAUGHING
DRAGON

At night George was lucky he had his shell to sleep in, for as Hojo slept tucked up in his blanket dreaming of his happy days in Japan, he laughed so much that he lit up like a lighthouse and sprinkled George with sparks.

Although Hojo missed Japan, George kept him from feeling miserable. Each day they lay in the sun and toasted homemade muffins. Hojo's breath was so warm that the island soon became covered in exotic flowers and migrating birds from Japan.

The birds were full of gossip. "The Japanese are having the worst winter for over one hundred years," they chirped. "Everyone is freezing, and there are icicles on the Emperor's toes." Hojo was very depressed. "If I could get back now I could keep my friends warm," he told George. "Only if you learn to control yourself," replied George. "You will have to practice breath control and try holding your breath. I will tell you sad stories to prevent you laughing."

As George told sad stories Hojo found he could hold his
breath quite easily, and slowly

. . . and fatter

. . . he got fatter   . . . and fatter

. . . until much to his surprise he floated up
into the air. "I can fly," shouted Hojo.

"You have turned
into a hot air balloon," exclaimed
George. "Now with the birds' help you
can fly to Japan if I can keep you from laughing." When Hojo
had been fitted with a basket to carry George they set off and
soon they were floating high above the clouds. "Try to hold
your breath until we are over land," shouted George as he
called out sad story after sad story.

Over Japan it was bitterly cold and the whole country was so deeply buried in snow that there was no sign of the Emperor or his Palace. To cheer Hojo up, George told him the joke about the cabbage with the cauliflower ears. Hojo laughed and as his hot breath escaped he became smaller and smaller until they drifted down onto the snow. George and the birds were glad they had Hojo's warm breath to protect them from the icy cold, and as George kept up a steady stream of jokes, the snow started to melt.

Before long, with George telling every joke he could think of, Hojo had melted a tunnel down to the Palace where the Emperor and his family were blue with cold. "We all missed you," said the Emperor, "and especially your hot breath."

Hojo quickly made some hot soup and had
everyone warm and happy before you could say
"Mareseatoatsandoeseatoats." "Thank goodness
no one asked for turtle soup," thought George.

Hojo was so happy he didn't stop laughing until winter had completely gone. As he melted the snow, the ground became covered in flowers, trees blossomed and birds sang in the branches. There were no more complaints from the courtiers and when one of them went past, George would call out, "A chuckle a day keeps the snow away."

The Emperor presented George with the Grand Imperial Medal and appointed him *Imperial Story-Teller and Breath-Controller* with the job of controlling Hojo's breath.

From that day on, Hojo's flames
were kept in check by George's stories,
but whenever he felt like a good laugh,
George told his funniest jokes and
Hojo put on a spectacular firework
display.

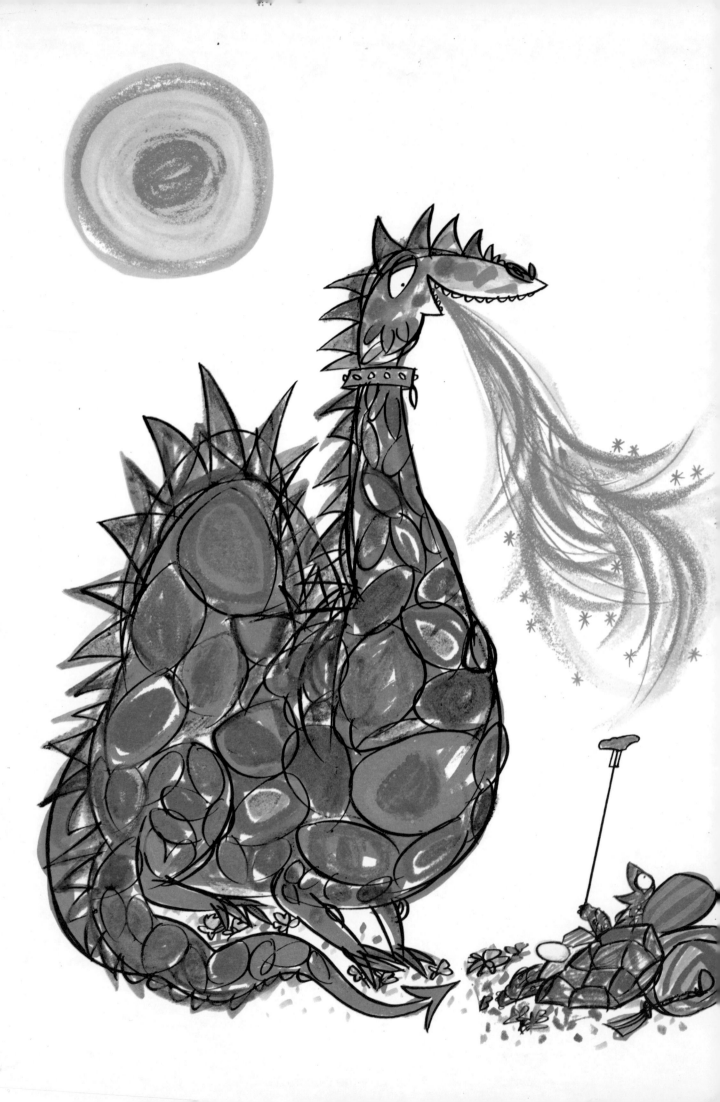